GOD'S WORLD

by
Sylvia Rouss

Illustrated by
Janet Zwebner

PITSPOPANY

NEW YORK ◆ JERUSALEM

GOD'S WORLD

Published by Pitspopany Press

Hard Cover ISBN: 1-932687-00-9
Soft Cover ISBN: 1-932687-01-7

Pitspopany Press titles may be purchased for fund raising programs
by schools and organizations by contacting:

Marketing Director, Pitspopany Press
40 East 78th Street, Suite 16D, New York, New York 10021
Tel: (800) 232-2931   Fax: (212) 472-6253
Email: pitspop@netvision.net.il
Website: www.pitspopany.com

Printed in Israel

To my children &
all the children in
God's World

SYLVIA ROUSS

"Where are we going, Mommy?" asks Eli, my wide-eyed, dimple-cheeked little boy. I smile as I lift him onto the child seat attached to the back of my bicycle.

"To God's world," I reply.

"But where is that?" Eli wonders aloud.

"You'll see," I answer, fastening the strap of the safety helmet under his chin. Eli coughs, his eyes water. Not from illness, but from the air around us.

We glance at the nearby factory smokestacks, Gray-black wisps of smoke float upward, darkening the sky. We listen to the blast of car horns, and smell the

fumes of early morning traffic. Slowly, I begin pedaling the bicycle out of the city, into the countryside.

Eli begins to sing a Hebrew song about the days of the week. His voice keeps pace with the rhythm of the turning bicycle wheels.

"*Yom Rishon, sunny day, Yom Shaynee, let's go play...*"

We pass by a small stream that has a warning sign — UNSAFE FOR SWIMMING AND FISHING! The murky waters were once home to rainbow-colored fish. And splashing children used to have such fun there. I continue to pedal while Eli sings.

"Yom Sh'leeshee, I want to try, Yom R'veeyee, to see the sky..."

On the ground, lying side by side in a

8

silent row, we notice freshly cut trees.
Above us, homeless birds hover, wondering
where to build their nests. And across
mounds of recently dug earth, a family of
squirrels scurries, like frightened refugees
searching for a safe place to live. I pedal
the bicycle onward. The air becomes
cleaner, the landscape fresher.

Eli sings, "*Yom Hameeshee, I want to run.
Yom Sheeshee, and have some fun...*"

Eli breathes easier. His eyes no longer water. He sings, "*Yom Shabbat...*" "We're here," I announce.

Eli sees the sign by the park entrance. He mouths the letters, "E-D-E-N." EDEN.

Hand in hand, we enter the gate. Eli looks with wonder at the breathtaking garden around him — Lush grass, leafy trees, blossoming flowers. The fragrant smell of mamosa fills us with joy.

"It's beautiful!" he exclaims.

"Yes," I nod in response. "Once the whole world looked like this park. This is the world God created."

"Tell me about it," Eli asks. "Tell me about God's World."

"Alright," I answer, unfolding a large blanket I have brought. "Close your eyes," I say to him. I drape the blanket over both our heads.

"In the beginning there was nothing but darkness.

"Now open your eyes," I tell him. Eli can't see me but I know he senses my presence.

I softly murmur, "Before there was a world, there was nothing but God. On Yom Rishon, the first day, God created the light."

I swiftly pull the blanket away. Eli blinks as his eyes adjust to the bright daylight.

"God divided the light from the darkness, and found it pleasing. The light God called Day, and the darkness, Night."

"On Yom Shaynee, the second day, God created the Heavens."

I spread the blanket on the grass. "Come," I say, taking Eli's little hand in my own. "Lie

16

down here next to me."
    We look upward at the puffy white clouds.

Dreamily, we watch them sail across an ocean of blue sky.

"On Yom Sh'leeshee, the third day, God created the land and the seas."
I remove my shoes and help Eli unlace his.

"God covered the land with grasses and trees," I continue softly, leading my barefoot son across the thick grass.

"It tickles!" giggles Eli, happily.
  "And God saw that it was very good,"
I laugh.

"On Yom R'veeyee, the fourth day, God created the sun, the moon, and the stars."

I sigh, gazing skyward. Eli lets the warmth of the sun wash over him. Little

beads of wetness form on his upper lip. He smiles at me as he licks away the saltiness.

"And God saw that it was good," I say smiling back.

"On Yom Hameeshee, the fifth day, God created the birds and the fish," I tell Eli as we walk to a little stream. He dips his toes in the cold water, startling a tiny fish.

22

A chirping sound draws my son's attention to a little bird flying overhead. Eli claps his hands with delight.

"And God saw that it was good!" I exclaim.

"On Yom Sheeshee, the sixth day, God created all the animals, and then the first people, Adam and Eve."

Eli and I marvel at our reflection in the clear stream. Suddenly, a huge croaking bullfrog leaps onto a lily pad, splashing us

both with water. I look at my son and we both begin laughing.

"And God saw that it was good," I chuckle.

"On Yom Shabbat, the seventh day, God was happy with Creation, and decided to rest. God blessed the day and called it Holy."

I lift my yawning child and carry him back to the blanket. Gently, I place Eli on the blanket and curl up beside him. With a protective arm around my sleeping son,

I close my eyes, and under a canopy of trees, we nap together. A soft breeze stirs us awake.

"It's time to go back," I whisper to my still drowsy child.

"Can't we stay here?" he pleads. "Do we have to go back?"

"Yes," I nod. "It's time for us to go home."

"But I like the world God created!" he insists.

"Our home was like this once," I patiently explain. "We were supposed to take care of His world, but people didn't listen."

"Can we change the world back to the way God created it?" asks Eli.

"Yes," I assure him. "With a lot of hard work."

"But I'm just a little boy," he reminds me. "What can I do?"

"You can lead the way," I tell him. "When you see litter, throw it in the trash. After you wash up, turn the faucet off. Take used bottles and paper to the recycle bin. This is just a beginning. As you grow, you'll learn to do more. When people see how careful you are to keep our world clean and beautiful, they will follow your lead. Then we will once again have the world God made for us."

I lift Eli onto the bicycle. I fasten his helmet strap under his chin. As I begin pedaling back to the city, my child sings softly —
"*Yom Rishon, there is a way, Yom Shaynee, to save the day. Yom Sh'leeshee,* let's show we care, *Yom R'veeyee,* and do our share. *Yom Hameeshee, let's give the earth, Yom Sheeshee, a new rebirth. Yom Shabbat, I hope and pray to see God's World again someday.*"